S0-AGK-635

THE LOVE BUG

THE LOVE BUG

Adapted by Scott Sorrentino
Based on the Screenplay by Bill Walsh and Don DaGradi
Based on the Story by Gordon Buford

114 Fifth Avenue
New York, New York 10011-5690

Copyright © 1997 by Disney Enterprises, Inc.

All rights reserved. No part of this book may be reproduced or
transmitted in any form or by any means, electronic or mechanical,
including photocopying, recording, or by any information storage
and retrieval system, without written permission from the publisher.
For information address Disney Press, 114 Fifth Avenue,
New York, New York 10011-5690.

Printed in the United States of America.

First Edition

1 3 5 7 9 10 8 6 4 2

The text for this book is set in 12.5-point Berkeley Medium.

Library of Congress Catalog Card Number: 97-80150

ISBN: 0-7868-4211-3

CHAPTER ONE

"How come no one's picking that one?" asked Roddy.

"'Cause it's a piece of junk," Hank replied.

Hank Cooper ran a hand through his thick brown hair and looked at the little broken-down Volkswagen Bug. Thirty years ago, maybe it had been a great car. Now it looked almost sad, as if it knew that it was old and out-of-date. Even its white paint was fading to a pale gray.

His friend Roddy considered the car again. On the surface, it did look like a piece of junk, but Roddy didn't care about looks. He didn't even care about his own looks. His reddish hair was always flying this way and that. He hardly ever shaved. It was the inside of things that mattered to Roddy. He was an artist after all, not a mechanic. The only reason he worked at a garage was for the spare parts. He sensed that there was something more than gears, fans, and belts inside this little car.

It was true that Herbie had seen better days. Many years ago, with Jim Douglas as his friend and driver, Herbie had traveled the world and won more than his share of the world's great auto races. Those were the good old days, Herbie thought. He wondered if he would ever have a special owner like that again. Then, suddenly, he made head-lamp contact with Hank.

"*Eerrrreeep,*" Herbie bleated, rattling his frame slightly. He was trying to get Hank's attention.

Hank thought he heard the car call to him, but that was ridiculous. He was imagining things. It was strange, though. He felt a sudden connection to the little car, as if they had something in common. Maybe it was the fact that they were both washed up. There was no denying it. Hank was just another former race-car driver living out the rest of his days as an auto mechanic. The closest he was ever going to get to competition was this Fix-Off Contest, which he would never have entered if he hadn't been forced to by his boss, Chuck, who owned the garage where he worked.

The contest was simple. Each mechanic drew a number. When your number was called, you chose a car from the selection of junkers and tried to fix it. Two hours later, the cars were lined up on the speedway and you attempted to start the car and race it one lap around the track. The winner got to keep the car, but Hank knew that wasn't the reason Chuck had wanted him to enter. Chuck's Car Shop was a joke, and everyone knew it, including Chuck. But Chuck figured if Hank could win this contest, people might want to have their cars repaired by the "best and fastest mechanic around."

As the numbers were called out and the mechanics chose their cars, one by one they all passed by the little VW.

"It's like when you were a kid and they picked kickball teams," Roddy said, remembering.

Hank nodded. He knew exactly what Roddy was talking about.

"I was always picked last," Roddy continued. "And I really hated that."

That was it. Hank had made up his mind.

"NUMBER SEVEN," the announcer called out.

Hank took the number seven from his chest pocket. He looked at Roddy, patted him on the shoulder, and went straight to the little Volkswagen Bug with the red, white, and blue stripe down its center and the number fifty-three painted in a circle on its hood.

"I'll take this one," he announced.

There were more than a few laughs from the crowd, but Hank didn't care. He was going to fix this little car and he was going to race it around the track. He felt sure of it.

"Gentlemen, FIX YOUR ENGINES!" the announcer shouted as Chuck rushed in to check on his boys.

"What'd I miss?" he asked, a little out of breath. Roddy and Hank were about to open the rear hatch. Chuck looked at the little car disapprovingly. "You picked this?"

"All you said was I had to enter."

"I like him," Roddy added, reaching into the toolbox for a wrench. They popped the hatch and looked carefully at the car's insides. Chuck shook his head and walked away, mumbling to himself.

Hank took the wrench from Roddy and squatted down for a better view. After checking a few screws, he found one that was loose and started to tighten it.

"*EreeeeK*," Herbie squealed.

Hank and Roddy both heard it, but neither of them thought it could have come from the car.

Hank paused for a second, then tightened a little more.

"*EreeeeK!*"

Unless Hank was going crazy, the sound was definitely coming from the car. Maybe the car was ticklish, Hank thought. He looked at Roddy who shrugged. Hank shook his head and gave the wrench a hard turn.

"*EREEEEK! RE-EREEEEK!*"

"I think he said the distributor," Roddy translated.

Hank shot him a look and Roddy shrugged, "That's what it sounded like."

"Oh, did it?"

Hank moved in to take a closer look.

"Well," he said, fumbling around inside the mess of metal, hoses, and caps. "The distributor's—cracked."

"See? He was right." Roddy patted the car on the fender. "You're gonna be okay," he said, affectionately.

Herbie blinked his headlights happily, and oddly enough Roddy didn't seem surprised at all.

Two hours later, the cars were assembled on the racetrack with their mechanics standing at their side. It was the moment of truth for the little VW.

"So here we go!" shouted the announcer. "Let's meet our panel of distinguished judges. First, from Shotz Specialty Autos, master of the custom car, Donny Shotz!"

A wacky-looking silver space-car came to a screeching stop in front of the announcer's platform and as the gullwing driver's-side door opened, out stepped Donny Shotz, a cigar-chompin', cowboy-boots-a-mile-high, ten-gallon-hat-wearing, wanna-be cowboy, smiling and waving like a fifty-foot flag on the Fourth of July.

"Second, from the Moore family of Modified Motorworks, it's Team Triple M driver, Simon Moore III!"

Simon Moore, stylishly dressed in a black Calvin Klein sport suit, stepped forward. Accompanied by his girlfriend-for-the-day, Veronica, and reeking of "*Eau* de some French guy" cologne, Simon grinned and waved, acknowledging the very slight applause.

"Please, control yourselves," he announced in a dramatic Scottish accent.

"And finally, from *Car and Track* magazine, Alex Davis!"

Now that was a name that Hank recognized immediately. He stopped what he was doing and looked over at Alex.

"Know her?" Roddy asked.

"Dated her," Hank replied.

Herbie heard that and turned his lights toward Alex. She was pretty, which he acknowledged with a spirited whistle.

Hank couldn't remember why he and Alex had broken up, and it didn't matter now. He had work to do.

"Wait, I know that mechanic," Alex said, spotting Hank for the first time.

Simon glanced quickly at Hank but was almost immediately distracted by the sight of the little Volkswagen.

"And I know that car," he said, frowning.

Up until two months ago, that little car had been Simon's, and he had raced it without success. His assistant, Rupert, had purchased the car at an auction, paying a fortune for it because it was Herbie, the famous car Jim Douglas had driven to win the Grand Prix in Monte Carlo and just about every other Formula One event. If that car had been the life force of Jim Douglas, it had been the death of Simon Moore. The last time Simon had raced he had finished dead last. Simon had never been so embarrassed in his career and promptly ordered the car sent to the junkyard. Now, here it was again. Just looking at

7

it gave him an ache in the pit of his stomach. He really hated that car. But before he could get too upset, his thoughts were interrupted by a burst of feedback.

"This is it, ladies and gents!" the announcer wailed into his cheap megaphone. "It's one lap around the track to see who's the best. Gentlemen, ATTEMPT TO START YOUR ENGINES!"

One of the cars immediately caught fire. Another car collapsed. A third car popped its hood ten feet into the air. There was steam, hissing, and smoke all around. Even Hank was having trouble. He turned the key forcefully again and again, and Herbie coughed and hiccuped, but the old VW wouldn't turn over.

"One . . . two . . . THREE!" cried the announcer as a green flag was waved to signal the start of the race.

A few of the cars actually started and began to make their way down the track. Hank watched them go by and renewed his efforts. Nothing.

"Get those dead cars off the track before the others come around," demanded the announcer.

Suddenly, a tow truck appeared in Hank's rearview mirror. There wasn't much time now. He stroked the dashboard reassuringly.

"Love to see you kick some tailpipe," he said. "We could both use a bit of a boost here."

Then, suddenly, as if propelled by rocket boosters, Herbie stood up on his hind wheels and roared away.

"WHOA!" Hank cried, grabbing at the seat to steady himself.

And Herbie, much to the surprise of everyone, held his wheelie as he raced down the speedway, passing cars left and right. When he finally put all four wheels on the ground there was only one car ahead of him.

"No problem," Hank said to himself. He adjusted his seat belt, wiped the sweat from his brow, and tightened his grip on the steering wheel.

Speeding around the final turn, Hank and Herbie easily passed the last car and raced through the finish line like champions.

"We have a winner!" the announcer broadcast.

Hank was grinning wildly. He got out of the car and waved to the cheering crowd, who were now standing on their feet.

"Congratulations to Hank Cooper, from Chuck's Car Shop," the announcer said, placing a radiator-hose wreath around his neck, "this year's best and fastest mechanic around!"

Hank raised his fist in triumph as the announcer handed him a giant silver wrench.

"Thanks," Hank said, as Roddy and Chuck came over to congratulate him.

"Great job!" Chuck said, patting him on the back.

"See, I knew that little car was a winner," Roddy added.

"The judges want to meet you," the announcer said, pulling Hank away.

"Gotta go meet some judges," Hank said, waving to Roddy and Chuck. First in line was Donny Shotz.

"I've never seen such a tiny car do such huge things," Donny said, removing the cigar from his mouth. "You must be one primo mechanic. We got some things to talk about. I'm gonna give you a call, okay?

With a chuckle and a painful smack on the back, Donny was off before Hank could respond. Next was Simon.

"I happen to know your car," he started, the accent almost disguising his rude nature, "and I don't believe what I just saw."

"Well, believe it," Hank said, almost convincingly. "I fixed it, then I just drove the you-know-what out of it."

Hank knew Simon from the circuit, but Simon didn't seem to recognize him.

"You don't remember me, do you?" Hank asked after a long pause. "I used to drive Formula One. We used to race together."

Simon just stared at him blankly. "We used to what?"

"Race. I was a driver. Hank Cooper?"

"Cooper? Cooper . . ." Simon thought for a moment, then shook his head. "Can't place it. Sorry. You never won against me, did you?"

"Well, no . . . but . . ."

"Ah, well, there you have it. But look at you, now," he said, grinning. "You've found something you're good at. Keep it up." And with a pat on Hank's back, Simon, too, walked away, snickering to himself.

Finally, there was Alex.

"Don't tell me *you* don't remember me?" Hank asked.

"Sure, I remember you. The love of my life. Or was it just a month?"

This was obviously not going to be a happy reunion.

"All I know," Alex continued, "is that your car shouldn't be able to do what it did, so I don't know *what's* going on."

That said, Alex brushed past Hank and left almost as quickly as she had arrived. Somewhat confused, Hank turned and addressed the little VW.

"Man, if this is how winners get treated," he told Herbie, "I'm going back to losing."

CHAPTER TWO

Later, after looking carefully at the car for anything unusual that might explain all of the things
that had happened, Hank shrugged, climbed
inside, and drove off. The speedway was almost
empty now, except for Alex, who was getting into
her slick red Porsche when Hank pulled up
alongside her.

"Hey lady," he called out. "Nice car."

She pretended not to hear, putting on her seat
belt and adjusting her rearview mirror.

"I want to ask you something," he persisted.

She glanced over at him and rolled her eyes.
"As long as it's not about us."

"No, it's about how come no one believes I
drove this stupid car one stupid lap around a
track."

"Because you started the lap with a standing start wheelie, which, given the horsepower-to-weight ratio of that car, is impossible."

"Maybe I fixed it up a little," he said, a little irritated. "Plus, I *can* drive, you know."

"Okay," she said, getting out of her car and walking to Herbie's passenger side. She opened the door and got in. "Let's see what you can do, Mr. 'Best and Fastest Mechanic'—and this better be good!"

"Whoa!" Hank cried as Herbie screeched to a stop just as the light turned red. "Isn't the gas pedal supposed to . . ." He stopped. It sounded too crazy. But he was sure that he had stepped on the gas to beat the yellow, not on the brake.

"What?" Alex asked.

"Nothing, it's just that . . ."

Suddenly a low-riding Cadillac convertible pulled up alongside them and stopped. It was thumping with the latest hip-hop music turned up full blast. The two boys inside were wearing sunglasses so dark that Hank wondered if they could see anything at all. They turned to look at Herbie, then inside at Alex and Hank, who smiled back nervously. Hank even added a half-wave.

"Hello," he said awkwardly.

The boys did not acknowledge him. Instead, one of them flipped a switch on the dash, and to Alex and Hank's surprise, their car began to bounce violently up and down. It went up, then down, then quickly up again. One side lowered itself, then the other side. Then it shot up quickly again. The rear jumped and settled, and then the front jumped. Up and down, back and forth, side to side. It was unbelievable! And then, for the finale, the entire car jacked itself up several feet and rotated back down, each side lowering itself independently.

Alex and Hank watched in amazement as the car finally came to rest and the boys looked over at them as if issuing a challenge. Hank could only shrug. There wasn't much a VW Bug could do to match that! No ordinary VW Bug, that is.

Suddenly, Herbie began to bounce up and down, causing Alex and Hank to immediately reach for the sides of the car and each other to steady themselves. After a moment's pause, as Hank and Alex realized they were holding each other and decided to grab onto something else, Herbie began to dance. Almost perfectly in synch with the music pounding from the Cadillac, Herbie jacked up and down, bounced side to side, boosted front, boosted back, sank to the ground, then shot back up again. He rocked back and forth, dipped, shot up, hopped, dove forward, and lifted up again. For his finale, he shot up five feet off his wheels, hung suspended in the air, then dropped to the ground with a happy bounce, settling with a sustained hiss.

The boys in the Cadillac stood up in their seats and applauded.

"*REEEP RU,*" Herbie bleated, taking a slight bow. Hank and Alex just looked at each other in amazement.

"When did you rig it to do that?" Alex asked.

Hank gulped. "I didn't."

"I was afraid you were gonna say that."

Alex was getting nervous now, but before she could even collect her thoughts, the windows rolled up, the doors locked and Herbie skidded away, burning rubber across the intersection and sending them flying backward in their seats.

"What's going on here?" Alex asked, thrown against the window by a sudden turn.

"I don't know. It's like . . . the car's . . ."

Herbie raced ahead, accelerating toward the turnoff for Seabreeze Point, a romantic spot where young lovers gathered in their cars on Friday and Saturday nights. During the day, though, it was just another winding, narrow mountain road, and they were going too fast for the kind of turns that lay ahead.

"Look, you don't have to impress me, I believe you can drive," Alex said, her voice shaking. "In fact, why don't you just stop right here, okay?"

Obviously she didn't notice that Hank had been stepping on the brake for the last mile or so. But the car wasn't stopping.

"I . . . I can't!" he shouted.

Then they both saw the sign.

"DANGER! ROAD OUT!" Alex and Hank screamed together.

Herbie was headed right for a cliff, but he knew better than to scare his new friends on their first date in a long while. Completely in control, he threw himself into a 360 and skidded to a stop with his rear wheels inches from the edge.

"*Reeeeeep!*" Herbie bleated, impressed by his driving skill.

"Let me out of here!" Alex shouted, fumbling with the door handle. It was locked. "Unlock this door!"

Hank tried his door, but it too was locked.

"They're locked, okay. Just take it easy. Settle down."

Alex sighed. "All right, just open it."

"I'm not keeping it closed."

"Yeah, like you didn't pop that wheelie and you didn't race up this road. Open the door NOW."

Hank reached over and tried the door. Nothing.

"Look, it's not like we're stuck. We can always roll down the windows and climb out. So let's just calm down."

"All right. As long as were calming down, why don't we talk about us now."

"I thought you didn't want to talk about us."

"Changed my mind. How 'bout telling me why you didn't want to go out with me anymore."

Their eyes met suddenly, and Hank was caught off guard.

"I'm sure I can get this door open," he said, fumbling again with the lock.

"Look, it's not like I didn't get on with my life. I just want to know why."

"Okay, okay," he said, finally. "I didn't want to go out with you anymore because you were always talking about racing. And not just about racing, but about *my* racing. And not just about my racing, but about my *bad* racing, about every missed shift, every blown engine, every crash."

"Well sorry, but you did basically wipe out every car you drove. I thought it was kinda funny."

"Let me give you a little dating tip, missy. Don't tell a guy his life's ambition is 'funny.'"

"Look, I liked you!"

"Yeah well I liked you, too! SO THERE!"

Embarrassed, Hank let his eyes wander, eventually turning his head toward the back seat.

"What are you doing?" Alex asked.

"Looking for the ejector seat."

Satisfied that his first matchmaking effort had been successful, Herbie started up and put himself in gear. Only a couple on the verge of love could irritate each other like that. With a contented bleat, Herbie headed back to the speedway, where Alex's car was patiently waiting. Mission accomplished, as far as Herbie was concerned.

Simon Moore's office at Moore Modified Motorworks was larger than any office needed to be. It was decorated with strange chrome sculptures and abstract silver and black paintings. And every picture on Simon's huge, glass desk was of himself.

As Simon sat admiring an eight-by-ten of one of his many racing victories, his assistant, Rupert, entered and came forward.

Rupert admired his boss. Deep inside, he wanted to *be* Simon. He even dressed like Simon, though for some reason Simon always looked better.

"What happened to that car you got rid of?" Simon asked.

Rupert's forehead wrinkled with confusion.

"The VW Bug that won the Fix-Off Contest," Simon explained.

"But you hate that car," he said.

"Yes," Simon said, wincing, "but I saw it do some rather amazing things that it never did while I had it. I know what cars can and can't do, and this car seems to do whatever it wants, and I want to know why. So find out the location of its garage. It had an idiot's name, 'Chick's' or 'Chack's' or—'CHUCK'S.' Yes, that's it! Find it."

"C'mere," Chuck said, ushering Hank through the garage. "I want you to see this."

Chuck's Car Shop wasn't much to look at, and Hank really didn't know what he was supposed to be looking for, but when they finally reached the main part of the garage, it was obvious that something was very different about the place. It was full of cars—cars that needed to be fixed. And there was a line of cars outside waiting to get in.

"Take a look." Chuck said, beaming. "You did this!"

"We can't handle all the work," one of the mechanics said.

"You can't handle *any* work," Chuck replied. Then he turned to Hank. "But what does it matter. You've brought honor to our humble garage."

"Yeah," Roddy added. "You guys were great."

"You guys?" Hank asked.

"You . . . and the little car here." Roddy gestured to the little VW.

"Since when do you like cars?" Chuck asked.

"Don't. But I like this one. Besides, I think he digs it here."

"Oh really, did he tell you that?" Hank asked.

Herbie blinked his parking lights in agreement.

"In so many words," Roddy replied.

"One more thing, Hank," Chuck said, patting Hank on the back. "I'm going to give you a raise."

"You don't have to do that, Chuck."

"Yes I do. Because that space-car guy called and wants to offer you a job with this new racing team he's starting. I'm giving you a raise so you can turn him down."

"What?" Hank was a little overwhelmed. "You didn't tell him anything, did you?"

"I said you'd think about it."

The phone was ringing, and one of the other mechanics ran to pick it up.

"Great!" Chuck said. "Another job offer for Hank."

"It's Alex, from *Car and Track*. For Hank."

"I thought she hated you," Chuck said, walking into his office.

"She does," Hank shouted after him. "But she loves my car."

Later that evening, Alex came to the garage to meet Hank for dinner—and to see the car.

"Hello again," Hank said, smiling at Alex.

"Hello again yourself."

Alex was wearing a shiny black, sleeveless dress, but Hank hardly had time to admire it before she walked past him toward Herbie.

"This is kind of embarassing," Alex said, studying the little VW, "but I just haven't been able to stop thinking about this car. I'm even thinking my magazine could do a piece on it."

Roddy appeared from behind one of his sculptures made primarily of radiator hoses.

"An article on Herbie," he said. "I like it."

"His name's Herbie," Alex added. "I like *that*."

"I like how the crazy artist knows the

car's got a name. Go ahead," Hank said to Alex. "Ask him."

"How do you . . ."

"He told me," Roddy interrupted. "And it's inscribed in a plate under his hood. I'm not deranged, y'know."

Hank threw him a doubtful look.

"Look, we gotta get going," Hank said. He turned and pulled Alex along with him.

"Wait," Alex said, stopping him. "Aren't we going to take Herbie?"

"You should," Roddy said. "He needs to get out, too. And he likes you, Hank. He thinks you're special."

"Well, that's very nice," Hank said, nodding at the car. "Thank you." He paused. "Wait, now *I'm* talking to the car."

"That's right. 'Cause he's alive. Remember, he has *feelings.*"

As Hank and Roddy continued arguing, Alex knelt down and put a gentle hand on Herbie's fender. Herbie purred, blinking his lights in appreciation.

"Did you see that?" Alex jumped up, stopping Hank and Roddy's argument. She tried to think of what to say next, but couldn't. If Hank hadn't seen it, he definitely wasn't going to believe it. "Well," she said as if nothing had happenend. "We can take my car. It's no Herbie . . . ," she confessed.

"I know," Hank said sarcastically. "It's a Porsche." Then, changing gears, he said, "I hope you don't mind, but Roddy here's got an art show tonight and I promised him we'd stop by."

Alex nodded, but her attention was still firmly fixed on the car, so Hank grabbed her hand impatiently and pulled her away.

"We'll see you at the show, Rod," he said, nearly running to the door.

"Wait," Alex complained as she was being whisked away. "I just want to check one more . . ."

Her voice trailed off and Roddy was left standing alone with Herbie.

"*Eerrrrrreeeep*," Herbie bleated sadly.

"He doesn't mean it," Roddy said, reassuringly. "He'll come around."

"*Reeep!*" Herbie beeped hopefully.

Then Roddy had an idea.

"How about if you come with me," he suggested.

"*Ereeeeep!*" Herbie replied enthusiastically.

Roddy smiled. "Definitely. You should definitely come with me."

CHAPTER THREE

The show was called "Vehiculart," which was no surprise at all to anyone who knew Roddy. What *was* surprising was the large display featuring none other than Herbie, which Hank and Alex noticed immediately as they walked in.

Herbie was secured on a large platform, with words like *Gridlock*, *Caution*, *Crash*, and *Speed* bouncing off him in bright neon. Roddy beamed as various artist-types came up to him and congratulated him.

Unfortunately, Hank did not qualify as an artist-type, nor was he in the mood to offer his congratulations.

"What's going on here, Rod?" he asked, a little annoyed. "Why's the car here?"

"I told you I thought he should get out. He's perfect for this."

"Y'know," Alex interrupted, "I think he looks pretty good here."

"*Reeeep ru*," Herbie beeped. He blinked his lights graciously.

"That's clever how you rigged him to respond to voices," Alex said to Roddy. "I like that."

Roddy looked confused. "I didn't rig him to do anything."

"But . . ."

"Why don't we go upstairs," Hank suggested, pulling Alex away. "Let's leave Roddy alone with his art."

As they hurried away, they didn't notice Simon Moore making his way through the crowd. He approached the car cautiously, peering inside. He eventually attracted Roddy's attention.

"Can I help you with something?" Roddy asked as Simon pressed his face against the driver's side window.

When Simon turned, Roddy recognized him immediately.

"You're the judge from the contest, aren't you?"

"Yes. I was hoping to take a closer look. Do you mind?"

Just then another artist-type stepped in front of Simon and began talking to Roddy. With Roddy preoccupied, Simon intended to investigate further. Herbie knew that Simon was up to no good, and he shuddered and shook with fear.

Meanwhile, Alex and Hank were watching the party from the loft above, bickering a lot, like they had been doing all evening.

"I just can't stop thinking about that car," Alex said.

"I know, I know. Geez, can't we talk about something else?"

"You're jealous—aren't you?"

"Whaddaya mean jealous?"

"Of Herbie. Of all the attention he's getting."

"Look, we don't have to be so observant. We can just chat, okay?"

"Face it, Hank. Herbie's an amazing little car. He does wheelies, jacks himself up and down, does one hundred miles per hour on four cylinders . . ."

"And of course we all know Hank can't drive. All Hank can do is crash."

"I didn't say that."

"Well I wish you would. At least it'd be something about me instead of something about my car."

Something was going on downstairs, and

Hank and Alex looked over the railing to see what all the commotion was about. It looked like Roddy was chasing someone around Herbie.

"Wait here," Hank said, hurrying down the stairs.

"Get out of the car! I mean it!" Roddy was shouting at Simon, who had locked himself in the car and was searching under the steering column.

He didn't know what he was looking for, but he knew there must be something that made this car so special. He opened the ashtray, but before he could see inside it shut quickly by itself. Then to his great surprise, he noticed that the key was still in the ignition. As Roddy banged on the window, Simon slipped the key into his pocket. Suddenly, the door unlocked and opened just as Hank arrived. Hank grabbed Simon by the collar and dragged him out of the car.

"Well, well," Simon proclaimed. "Cooper, isn't it?"

"You know exactly who I am," Hank threatened, pushing Simon against the door. "Now what are you doing in my car."

"Just trying to see how it's been modified, because it couldn't have done what I've seen it do . . . especially given its driver."

When Hank chooses Herbie in the Fix-Off contest, he gets more repair help than he expected.

"Okay, little car, let's see what you've got under the hood," Hank says to
Herbie.

When Hank wins the Fix-Off contest, he gains instant popularity . . . and many new customers for Chuck's Car Shop.

"Say Her-bieeeeee."

Jim Douglas says hi to his old friend.

Alex gains firsthand racing knowledge for her article on Herbie.

Herbie faces some serious competition from Horace, the Hate Bug.

Hank aptly names Herbie "The Love Bug."

"Oh yeah, well let me tell you something about driving," Hank growled, starting toward Simon as Roddy tried to hold him back.

"I'm really frightened, Cooper," Simon snarled. "I'm shaking in my boots."

Simon stood right in front of Herbie, who knew what he had to do. He released his hood, which made swift and painful contact with Simon's jaw, snapping his head up and back. Simon fell into the open hood and as he nursed his swelling jaw, he couldn't help noticing the large silver-engraved plate directly in front of his face. He was still in a lot of pain, but he managed to concentrate long enough to make a mental note. Engraved in the plate were Herbie's name, some other words in German, and then another name: DOKTOR GUSTAV STUMPFEL.

Seconds later, Hank pulled him out from under the hood and stood him up.

"You're outta here," Hank said, pushing Simon toward the door.

"Fine," Simon said, casually. "I have what I need."

When he was out of view, he reached into his coat pocket for his cell phone and dialed.

"Rupert," he commanded. "I want you to find a German engineer named Gustav Stumpfel.

Yes, Stumpfel. It's not your place to ask why. Just do it!"

He closed the phone and put it back in his coat pocket. As he hurried out of the building, he bumped into Chuck, who was just arriving. The crowd was still murmuring about the recent disturbance, and Chuck sensed that something had just happened. He looked around curiously.

"What'd I miss?"

Back at Moore Modified Motorworks, there was a lot of buzz surrounding the arrival of Dr. Stumpfel, a gray-haired man who bore a slight resemblance to Albert Einstein. He told Simon the story of how fifty years earlier he had been part of a team of engineers working for the German government to create a new kind of car. They had called it the "people's car": an automobile that was easy to drive and easy to maintain. Plans were drawn, but with the outbreak of World War II, the car was never made. After the war, the Americans, who had heard of the car, wanted one for themselves, and they brought him to the United States for questioning. But they had misunderstood. Somehow, they had translated "people's car" as "car person," which they assumed meant it was somehow "alive."

To avoid being sent back to Germany, the doctor told the Americans he could make the car, and using his original blueprints, he began to work. Of course, nothing could really make the car alive. Yet one day, by accident, a beautiful framed photograph of his beloved wife, Elsa, accidentally fell into the liquid metal vat. And that turned out to be the secret ingredient. The love that the doctor had for his wife was fused into the very materials of the car itself. As he neared completion, the doctor realized that Herbie was alive.

Fearing his discovery would be used for evil purposes, Dr. Stumpfel set the car free. Later, to his delight, he learned that Herbie had found a good home with Jim Douglas, a race-car driver, and was racing at events around the globe with great success. He never saw the car again, but still, hardly a day went by when he didn't think about his greatest triumph—Herbie, the living car.

"That's quite a story, Doctor," Simon said as the doctor wiped his glasses with a handkerchief. "The question is, how would you like to build another car just like it?"

"Well," the doctor began with an accent that suggested Germany more than California, "of course, I would love to."

Simon nodded at Rupert, who nodded back.

"But it is impossible. I would need materials, facilities . . ."

"You can use mine, of course," Simon offered.

Rupert helped the doctor out of his chair and they proceeded down a hallway to a pair of large doors. Stepping inside, Simon began to throw a series of switches. As the area lit up section by section, the doctor, to his amazement, found himself standing in the largest hangar he had ever seen, filled with all of the latest gadgetry, telemetry, and every other kind of "-try."

"So, doctor, can you make another car or not?"

"I think I can," he mumbled, his mouth still gaping open in astonishment. "I think I can. Of course, I will need a piece of metal from the original car."

"Will this do?" Simon asked, removing Herbie's key from his pocket. "It was a gift."

The doctor nodded. "And lastly I will need something from you. A photograph, perhaps, of someone you love."

"Someone I love. Did you hear that, Rupert? Quickly, get me a photo of someone I love."

Rupert looked at Simon blankly, not knowing

quite what to do, but he left anyway. He'd think of something.

"Yes, yes," Simon proclaimed, mostly to himself. "Perhaps we can throw a few other things into the mix as well. They think they have such a cute little car. Wait until they see *my* car."

Just as he began what promised to be a good, theatrical, villainous laugh, Rupert returned with a picture.

"Here you go, boss. Someone you love."

"What?" Simon said, skeptically. "I don't love . . ."

He looked at the picture and was pleasantly surprise.

"Well, very good, Rupert," he declared. "This should do quite nicely."

It was, of course, a picture of himself.

CHAPTER FOUR

"Roddy!" Hank called from Herbie's front seat. "Where's the key?"

"I dunno. It wasn't there last night after the show, either."

Donny Shotz had come to take a look at Herbie and maybe even give Hank a new job, so not being able to start the car was a big problem.

"If you didn't have the key, Roddy, how'd you get home?"

"Herbie drove."

Hank was afraid he would say that.

"Look," Donny started, "I really wanted to see the little car do its tricks. Maybe I should come back another time."

Hank got out of the car and took Donny aside. "Forget about the little car. I'm not gonna race *it*. I'm going to drive *your* cars."

"Who said anything about driving?"

Hank was confused. "Well, Chuck said that you were putting together a team, and that you needed—"

"I got plenty of drivers," Donny interruped. "What I need is a funny little joke car to entertain the line at the snack bar. You're just the mechanic."

Hank's face sunk. He blinked a few times and looked around at Chuck and Roddy.

"Oh," he said quietly.

After a moment, his eyes narrowed. "Well then," he burst out angrily, "you can take your snack bar and shove it!"

Donny was so surprised at the outburst that he almost swallowed his cigar. He looked like he wanted to say something, but all he could do was nod a few times and back out of the garage.

Hank was still fuming when Chuck came over and put a friendly hand on his shoulder.

"For what it's worth," he said sincerely, "I'm sorry."

"Yeah, well, it woulda come out eventually," Hank said, shaking his head. "Listen, I'm getting out of here."

"Outta here where?" Chuck asked.

"Don't know. Don't care. Anywhere there's

35

not some stupid little car taking credit for everything I do."

And with that, Hank turned and walked out of the garage. Chuck watched until he was out of sight, then lowered his head, turned and walked slowly into his office.

"Eereeeep reeeeer," Herbie whimpered.

Roddy put a reassuring hand on his fender.

"He'll be back," he said gently. "Don't worry about that."

Dr. Stumpfel had a look of horror on his face as he closed the doors behind him and turned around quickly, trying to catch his breath.

"The car must be destroyed!" he declared.

Simon smiled broadly. "So, you were able to build it!"

"Yes, yes, of course," the doctor gasped, his voice shaking. "But something went terribly wrong."

A loud growling sound could be heard coming from inside the hangar. It was the car, and only an evil car could produce such an angry, beastlike roar. The doctor shuddered at the thought, but Simon just continued to smile.

"Let's see it," he said.

The shop was closed and nobody seemed to be

around when Hank came by a few hours later.

"He's gone, Hank," Roddy said. He was staring blankly out the window and looked like he hadn't moved for hours. "He went out looking for you."

"What do you mean he went out looking for me?" Hank asked in disbelief. "By himself?"

Roddy approached his friend slowly and calmly.

"I know you think I'm whacked out," he started, "but this is real. Think about it." His eyes widened as he moved his face closer and closer to Hank's. "The wheelies. The locked doors. Heck, driving me home last night. Think about it. He's *alive*."

All this took a few moments for Hank to absorb. He turned away, then back again. He started to say something, then stopped.

"But . . ."

Roddy was nodding.

"So . . ." Hank stopped. "Well, if he's really alive . . ."

Hank wanted to believe, and Roddy knew he wanted to believe. But believing wasn't something that just happened. He knew that, too. To believe, you had to feel it deep down inside. And that was happening to Hank right now.

"Then I gotta find him!" Hank said, grabbing his jacket and running out of the garage.

This made Roddy very happy, and if Herbie had been there, he would have been happy, too.

With a thundering rumble, the huge steel barrier rose out of the floor revealing the silhouette of a car, smoke rising ominously around it.

"It's beautiful!" Simon gasped. He moved toward the car, admiring its sleek contours.

It was much more than a Bug, it was more like a black beetle, or something darker, deadlier. As Simon reached out to touch it, it snarled softly like a wild cat waiting to pounce.

He motioned for Rupert, who came rushing to his side. The doctor stood away, too afraid to get any closer.

"I think it's time to eliminate the competition," Simon said with doom in his voice.

"What about the doctor?" Rupert asked.

Simon thought for a moment. "Cut him loose," he said.

Rupert nodded and left Simon basking in the evil glory of this, his most prized possession. The car was made for him. In a sense, it was made out of him. They were one.

* * *

Herbie wandered the streets for hours looking for any signs of Hank, yet with each turn he found that he was only driving further and further away. He called out, but there were no answers. And yet he didn't give up hope. He wouldn't rest until Hank knew how special he was. He wanted Hank to know that everything was going to be okay.

Hank was looking for Herbie. At least once he thought he had heard that familiar bleat, but when he looked closely it was some other car. It wasn't Herbie. No other car was like Herbie. Why hadn't he believed sooner? This was all his fault, he thought. His only hope was that eventually Herbie would come back to the garage. But he wasn't about to give up, even though it was getting late. Herbie was out there somewhere, and Hank was determined to find him.

Herbie turned a corner and found himself in a dark alley. It was a dead end, so he tried to back up and turn around. Suddenly, he heard revving and growling. And it was getting louder. As he turned around, there in front of him was a vicious black car ready to attack, its wheels spinning smoke into the air.

Rupert got out of the car and shut the door.

"Sorry, little car," he said calmly. "This is the end of the line."

The black car raced forward, and Herbie backed up until he was pinned against the alley wall. His frame shuddered with fear, and he bleated nervously as the evil car cast its shadow over him.

With a roar the black car attacked Herbie, slamming him into the brick wall, and then backing up for more. Tires screeching, the beetle smashed into Herbie again and again, breaking every window and crushing Herbie's small frame into a twisted pile of metal. Herbie was no match for the bigger, more ruthless beetle. It was such an ugly scene, even Rupert had to turn away.

"Herbie! HERBIE!"

Hank cupped his hands around his mouth and continued to call out. It was really late now, and he had been all over town, at some places twice.

"HERRRRRBIEEEEE!" he called out again.

Then he heard something. It was faint, but it sounded like Herbie. It was coming from somewhere just ahead. Hank ran in the direction of the sound.

"Herbie?"

The bleating sounded more like crying now, and Hank's look turned from hopeful to worried as he rounded a corner and peered into the alley which seemed to be the source of the sound. He couldn't believe his eyes.

There in a heap in front of him was what was left of Herbie. His frame was bent beyond recognition, and every inch of him seemed to be dented or broken.

"Oh, Herbie," he said kneeling next to the car. "What did they do to you?"

He reached out and touched Herbie's fender. "What did *I* do to you?"

Herbie's headlamp began to flicker.

"You're gonna be okay," Hank said, reassuringly. "We'll fix you up. I promise."

"Eeeerrrrrrr," Herbie bleated one last time as his headlamp faded out completely.

Hank rested his head on the little car's fender. Suddenly, it was pitch dark in the alley, almost as dark as Hank felt within his heart.

It isn't every day you bury a car, but since Herbie had been *alive* it seemed the right thing to do. Roddy, Chuck, Alex, and Hank gathered at the cemetery with all of Herbie's parts in a large crate, ready to lower them into the ground.

As they each thought about Herbie and what he had meant to them, two men approached from the street nearby.

The first man was Dr. Stumpfel, whom none of them had ever met. The other distinguished-looking man was taller and a little younger.

"I'm Jim Douglas," he said, extending a consoling hand to Hank. "I was a friend of Herbie's. Mind if I take a look?"

Hank looked at Jim thoughtfully. "It's worse than you think."

"Don't worry, I've seen pretty bad."

Hank and Roddy opened the crate, and Jim and Dr. Stumpfel looked inside at the various pieces of Herbie, all twisted and bent.

"Aw, Herbie," Jim said, softly.

"My little car," the doctor added, sadly.

Hank and the others looked at the doctor, wondering who he was.

"Pardon me," Jim said, realizing the oversight. "This is Dr. Stumpfel. He built Herbie thirty years ago."

"Well, nice job," Hank said, leaning against the open crate. "He's amazing . . . or . . . was."

Hank looked at Jim, then at the doctor.

"And will be again," Jim said confidently.

"That'll be a good trick," Alex said.

"He's pretty far gone, Mr. Douglas," Roddy added.

The doctor, who had been thinking all along, suddenly spoke with a burst of enthusiasm.

"All we need," he began, "is a computerized metalwork factory with parts replication facilities."

"Fine," Hank said, shaking his head, "except all we have is Chuck's." He shot a look to Chuck. "Sorry, Chuck."

Chuck nodded, trying not to take it personally.

"But what're we even talking about?" Hank continued.

Suddenly, everyone's attention was focused on Jim.

"We're going to rebuild him," he said.

CHAPTER FIVE

It wasn't easy getting Donny Shotz's help, especially after Hank had told him off, but even forgiveness was possible if the price was right. Fixing Herbie was going to cost Hank all of the racing money he had been saving, but he knew it was worth it. Jim and Dr. Stumpfel said that only Herbie's original parts would work, and Donny was the only person around with the facilities necessary to reshape Herbie's twisted metal and make him new again.

Day and night they worked together on Herbie—Hank, Alex, Jim, and Chuck. Even Roddy got involved, painting the panels as they arrived from Donny's factory. Things seemed to be moving along nicely.

One afternoon, after several long hours of

welding, Hank, Alex, and Jim found themselves sitting together talking about Herbie.

"What was he like when you knew him?" Alex asked.

"Everything we'd like ourselves to be," Jim said without hesitation. "Loyal. Giving. Pure."

"I just wish I'd figured that out before," Hank said, regretfully.

"He'd understand," Jim said frankly. "That's probably what he's best at, understanding. That, and soaking up his owner's personality, and then giving it back."

Neither Hank nor Alex seemed to understand.

"He becomes like his owner," Jim explained. "And helps them get what they want."

Alex looked at Hank playfully. "So, the other day, it wasn't *Herbie* that whipped up to that secluded spot and locked the doors and all that. It was you who wanted to get me alone."

Hank was a little embarrassed. "What? Me? No . . . the car . . ."

Jim started to chuckle, then turned to Hank, smiling. "Herbie did that to me, too. That's how I met my wife."

He walked back to the workbench where some engine parts were awaiting his attention while Hank and Alex looked at each other awkwardly.

Hank was working all night without sleeping, eating only occasionally, and scarcely speaking a word. He was completely lost in the project of recreating Herbie.

"You didn't eat your fishwich," Roddy hollered to him, picking the half-eaten sandwich off the workbench.

"I'll get to it later."

"Special delivery!"

It was Donny followed by several men bringing various parts into the garage.

"Great. Just set them over there," Hank said, distracted. He was in the middle of soldering some molding onto one of the reformatted doors.

"Looks like you've made some progress," Donny said, impressed.

Hank nodded. "I'll get your money now."

As Hank started to leave, Donny reached for him and held him back. He could see that this was a labor of love, and for the first time in a long time, he was actually moved. "Don't worry about it. Get it to me later."

He patted Hank on the shoulder and

left. Without hesitation, Hank returned to his work.

Alex and Roddy watched from a distance as Hank continued working away.

"He's still at it," she said, concerned.

"Won't stop," Roddy replied.

When Alex, Chuck, Roddy, Jim, and Dr. Stumpfel arrived the next morning and opened the garage door, Hank was lying on the floor next to Herbie, who was covered with a large canvas. The light just about blinded him, and he rubbed his eyes; it looked like he hadn't even slept.

"Is there anything we can do?" Jim asked.

Hank stood up, shaking his head.

"Nope," he said, stretching. "Nothing can be done."

This prompted the doctor to rush over, consoling him. "Oh, my boy, you mustn't give up," he said, brushing some dirt off Hank's overalls.

"I'm not giving up," he said. "I'm finished!"

And with that, he pulled off the cover and revealed a fully assembled Herbie, painted and shining like brand new.

"I think you all know Herbie," he said, proudly.

They rushed in and crowded around the car.

"Herbie?" Roddy asked. "Are you there?" He leaned in close to the car, waiting for an answer. Nothing.

"Well," Alex asked, "is it the same car?"

"I dunno," Hank admitted. "And the stupid part is that we don't even have a key to find out."

This caught Jim's attention. He reached into his pocket and removed a shiny key, which sparkled in the glowing daylight. "I always kept a spare," he said. "Just for luck."

As he started to hand the key to Hank, Hank motioned for him to stop. "Please," Hank said, "the honor is yours."

Jim nodded graciously and stepped forward. He got in the car and looked around. Sitting behind the wheel of Herbie was like coming home to Jim, and he wanted to take just a moment to relive some of those great memories. They had shared some incredible adventures. Then, with a turn of the ignition, the car started, humming like it was just off the showroom floor.

Hank peered through the driver's side window and looked anxiously at Jim. "But is it . . . him?"

Herbie wasn't going to keep them in suspense any longer.

"*Reeep reeep! EerrrrEEEP!*" Herbie bleated

enthusiastically, sending cheers, hugs, and smiles all around. It was a great day for the crew at Chuck's Auto Shop and a great day for Herbie. For the first time in a long time, he felt good as new!

Simon Moore had the look of a man who had everything and didn't really know what to do with it. He had the greatest, most powerful car alive, he had eliminated the competition, and yet he was still unsatisfied. Were there no more worlds to conquer, he wondered?

Simon had named the car Horace, and Horace was, in a word, restless. He needed to get out. He needed to get some exercise. He needed to race.

"Okay, okay, my precious," Simon said as the car shuddered, chomping at the bit for some action.

"Rupert!"

And Rupert bounded in, eager to serve. "Yes, sir."

"Get my driving gear!"

As the others celebrated, Jim Douglas kneeled next to Herbie and spoke to him gently. "Well, pal," he said, "I think you're in the hands of some fine people here."

"Eeeerr," Herbie whirred.

"And yes, they do look good together."

Herbie and Jim looked over at Hank and Alex, who were pretending to toast each other with their coffee mugs. They were laughing, and for the first time, looked almost like a couple.

Jim smiled and stood up. "So I'll see you around," he said, giving Herbie one last pat on the fender and walking toward the garage door.

"Jim. What're you doing?" Hank asked, putting down his mug.

"It's time for me to go," Jim said, standing at the door.

"But what if we need you?"

"If you have any more questions," Jim said, walking down the driveway, "just ask Herbie. He'll know." He waved one last time, then disappeared.

Alex came over and put a hand on his shoulder.

"So, you think it's true?" she asked.

"That Herbie has all the answers?" Hank wasn't sure he knew what she meant.

"Noooo, that he's trying to get us back together. Because . . ."

"Well that's crazy," Hank said quickly.

"You bet it is," Alex agreed.

"Yep. Uh-huh." Their words began to overlap.

"Well, I'm just gonna get more coffee," she said, moving awkwardly away.

"Right. I'm just gonna . . . stay here."

As he watched her go, he kneeled down beside Herbie and looked him right in the headlamp. "If you *are* gunning for us, pal, you got your work cut out for you."

Even in full designer driving gear, Simon was having trouble controlling Horace the evil car. Swerving in and out of traffic, Simon had no idea where he was going, only that he wasn't, strictly speaking, driving.

"Hold on!" he shouted. "Slow down a bit, will you? Just exactly where are we—"

And they came to a screeching halt right in front of Chuck's Car Shop. Somehow the devil car had known that Herbie was still alive. It was clear he wanted a rematch.

"All right," Simon said, putting a lock on Horace so he would stay put. "I'm going to settle this once and for all."

"Where's Dr. Stumpfel?" Hank asked Roddy as they cleaned up the mess from their impromptu celebration.

"It's the strangest thing. He spoke about building something horrible, and how he had to burn some blueprints, then he left in a big hurry. I didn't know what he was talking about, but . . ."

"Knock, knock."

It was Simon, and he walked in uninvited, as unwelcome as any guest who had ever set foot in Chuck's garage.

"Well, well," Simon began, "if it isn't 'Home of the Nice People's Car.' What a perfectly ridiculous dump," he said, looking around.

Hank, Roddy, and Alex joined together, standing in front of Herbie as if protecting him from the dangerous Scot.

"I've come to offer you a chance to redeem yourself, Cooper."

"Redeem myself. How?"

"By racing again. Against my little car. To paraphrase your American westerns, there's not enough room in this town for two living cars. Whoever wins, gets to keep them both and do with them as he pleases."

Hank and Alex shared a concerned look.

"Now then," Simon continued, "Shall we say tomorrow—at dawn?"

Hank's lips curled into a worried smile.

"You make it sound like a *duel*."

Out of nowhere, Simon slapped Hank across the face with his leather gloves. Alex gasped.

"That's exactly what it is," Simon said, his face inches from Hank's. "And may the best car win."

CHAPTER SIX

If there was a physical definition of the middle of nowhere, this must be it, Hank thought, as he, Roddy, and Alex paced nervously back and forth. Team Herbie was all suited up in white jumpsuits with Herbie's familiar red, white, and blue vertical stripe. All suited up and nowhere to go—yet.

Just then Chuck pulled up in his tan El Camino and parked off to the side in the dirt.

"So, where is this jerk?" he asked no one in particular.

"Maybe he had second thoughts," Alex suggested, still pacing.

Suddenly, the sound of an approaching car caught their attention. Moments later, the evil black car skidded to a stop in front of the team and out stepped Rupert and Simon in black racing gear.

"Good morning," Simon said. "Ready to lose?"

Horace growled fiercely while Herbie shuddered and whined nervously.

"I see these two have met," Simon remarked.

Hank turned to Herbie and patted him reassuringly. "It's okay, Herb. We're here."

"Where did he get that car?" Alex asked.

"That's what the doctor meant," Roddy answered. "You know, when he said there was another Herbie."

"Please," Simon corrected, "he's not another Herbie. His name is Horace, and he's a vast improvement over your car."

The group ganged up and moved toward Simon, who immediately backed away.

"Now, now, curb your violence. That's not what this is about—yet. Now, the finish line is twenty miles through that pass there," he said, pointing. "I've arranged for the private use of this road, so you will see neither other cars, nor radar-wielding authority figures. There are no rules, of course, other than the loser loses his vehicle."

Alex looked at Hank, who looked at Herbie. They were all thinking the same thing.

"I can't wait to own you," Simon sneered,

looking at Herbie. "Horace is going to have such fun with you."

"Look, are we gonna race here, or what?"

As Hank and Simon stared each other down, Alex could only shrug and shake her head.

"This is such a guy thing," she said, disgusted.

Finally, Chuck stepped up to make himself known. "Somebody's gonna need to wave a flag or do a countdown or something—right?"

Simon snapped his fingers and Rupert dashed over with a yellow flag, which he handed to Chuck.

"I didn't actually mean me," Chuck said.

"I'll be waiting for you at the finish line, Cooper," Simon said, walking back to Horace. "Do hurry. Wouldn't want the tea to get cold."

He laughed and got into the car.

Herbie's team looked a little worried, except Hank, who turned to them and looked at each of them intently. "Okay gang," he announced. "Saddle up."

At the starting line, the two cars revved loudly, almost straining to contain themselves. Chuck stood ahead of them holding the yellow flag high in the air.

"One . . . two . . . THREE!" he shouted, lowering the flag as the cars sped past him, just barely clearing his stocky frame. He immediately turned around and watched them speeding off down the long, narrow road leading up into the nearby mountains. "GO, HERBIE, GO! GO!"

Soon both cars were out of sight.

"They're all gonna die," Chuck said to himself.

Back on the road, Herbie and Horace were neck and neck. They passed each other a few times, but mostly they were even with each other. Then Simon mockingly waved good-bye, and suddenly Horace shot ahead like a rocket. It was no contest.

"This is all too easy," Simon told Rupert as they watched Herbie fall further and further back in their rearview mirror.

"Boy can that car move," Alex said, watching Horace speed away.

"Yeah, well, he's being driven well," Hank complained. He was not enjoying this at all so far.

"Herbie's just holding back," Roddy offered. "Anytime now, he's gonna strike."

"Well," Hank wondered, "anytime would be nice—"

Herbie responded, rocketing them back into

their seats as the gas pedal kicked forward by itself. Within moments, they were right up against Horace once again. In fact, to their surprise, they zoomed right by him.

"Now that's more like it," Hank said, patting the dashboard.

"All right, car," Chuck said.

He was still stuck at the starting line, trying to get his old car to start.

"I take back all the things I've said about you over the years. I'll give you a wash this week, how about that—and a wax, too."

The car chugged, coughed, then almost started, but died again.

Herbie's lead was short-lived, as Horace pulled up once again alongside. This time, however, Hank was ready. He swerved and blocked Horace, forcing him back.

"Good move," Alex said. Hank smiled at her. That was the first time he ever remembered her complimenting his driving. He supposed he could get used to it.

But Horace was not to be denied. He pulled up on Herbie's other side and Hank couldn't hold him this time. Growling and grunting, Horace rammed into Herbie, sending him slightly off course.

"So, he wants to trade paint, does he?" Hank said. He jerked the wheel hard and slammed into Horace, who fell behind again.

"Rupert," Simon said, his fiery eyes raging. "I believe it's time to reveal the first 'modification.'"

Flipping a switch on the dash marked "Mod #1," a steel spoke was released from inside the right front wheel. Then, like magic, it spread open into a round series of spinning spikes.

Simon gunned the car forward and maneuvered right up alongside Herbie. The spikes were dangerously close, and Simon looked over at Hank and his crew and indicated the gadget with his eyes.

"Um, Hank?" Roddy cried.

"You gotta be kidding," Hank said, eyeing the spikes.

"I think this guy's seen too many James Bond movies," Alex cracked.

"Hey Hank," Roddy continued. "You gotta get away. I mean now!"

"I know, I know."

But it was too late. Simon swerved into Herbie and the spikes caught his rear tire, shredding it instantly and sending him spinning off the road into the dirt. By the time Hank was able to stop, Simon was already around the next curve and out of sight.

The doors flew open and the trio got out of the car, shaking their heads.

"Herbie!" Roddy cried. "Are you okay?" He looked at Alex. "We can probably fix this—can't we? Hank?"

But Hank had walked away, defeated. He threw down his helmet and stared off into the distance while Alex and Roddy exchanged concerned looks.

At the same time, Simon could not have been happier. "Well, that's that!" he proclaimed. "We've done it!"

"All right," Rupert howled. "So what happens now?"

"We celebrate."

Rupert knew exactly what that meant. "And guess who remembered to bring the boss's favorite sparkling apple cider?" he said, removing two overflowing glasses from underneath the glove compartment. "ME!"

"Look Hank," Roddy said, trying to be sympathetic, "if you're not gonna do anything about this, we will."

"Don't bother," Hank said over his shoulder. "The spare's flat. It's the one thing I didn't have time to fix."

Punctuated by an apologetic shrug, he walked back toward the car, his head lowered in shame.

"So that's it," Alex protested. "We're just done? Or is this where I'm supposed to give the big Suzy Cheerleader speech? Be the *rah-rah* adoring female?"

She rushed over to him and threw herself at him.

"Oh no, Hank," she cried mockingly, "you've got to go on. I believe in you, Hank." She stopped suddenly. "Is that what's supposed to happen now? Well forget it!" she said, turning away. "I can't believe after all this, you're just gonna quit!"

"You just don't understand," Hank explained. "Herbie's a friend of mine, and that guy's out there trying to kill him, okay, and I don't want to let that happen—not again."

"Well then," Alex said, finally getting it, "what are you going to do?"

"I have no idea."

But then, suddenly, he did have an idea.

"Wait a minute," Hank said, walking over to Herbie. "Maybe we should take Jim's advice and

61

ask Herbie. What do you say, pal?" he asked, bending down. "In or out?"

"Reeep reeep!" Herbie answered without hesitation.

"I'd say we're in," Hank announced.

"Except that the spare's still flat," Roddy said.

"That's right," Hank said, patting Roddy on the back. "And it's a good thing you're an artist."

"It is?"

Moments later, Hank tossed the shredded tire aside and replaced it with the flat spare, which he then began to fill with one of Roddy's spray paint bottles which they found in a box under Herbie's hood.

"Think it'll hold?" Roddy asked.

"No," Hank said dryly, "but it's the only chance we've got—if we're still in this race."

"Oh, we're in," Alex said, pointing to Horace who could still be seen driving casually through the pass. "They have no idea we're coming."

As they all scrambled to get back into the car, Hank and Alex bumped into each other, forcing an unexpected embrace. Alex looked up at Hank somewhat admiringly.

"So, the old Hank's back? Not the old quitting Hank, but the older one, the Hank who never gave up?"

"Yeah, I guess," he said, almost forgetting that he was still holding her.

She noticed his hands on her hips, and brought her arms around his shoulders.

"Good," she said, smiling, " 'cause he's the one I liked."

"You're a very confusing woman," he suggested. "You know that?"

"I try."

Then, without thinking, he just went for it, pulling her close and kissing her.

"REEEEEP REEER!" Herbie bleated happily. He knew he could get them together. He knew it all along.

As their lips parted, Hank smiled and looked into Alex's eyes. "Great Suzy Cheerleader speech, by the way."

"Oh, shut up," Alex said, playfully pushing him away.

And they all jumped into the car and sped off down the road, leaving a trail of dust and dirt.

"Think we can catch him?" Alex asked, her face showing signs of concern.

"We'll catch him, no problem," Hank said confidently. "I'm just worried about what happens when we do. . . ."

CHAPTER SEVEN

As Simon was regaling Rupert with yet another boring story of how he left one of his many fiancées standing at the altar, they hardly noticed Herbie speeding up behind them.

"What in the . . . ?"

Simon could hardly believe his eyes. "Well, if they refuse to lose gracefully, then they can die like slugs. Strap yourself in Rupert," he said, grinning. "It's time for modification number two."

With a flip of another switch labeled "Mod #2," a grenade launcher was deployed in the rear of the car, ready to fire.

"Look out!" Alex screamed, as a small object shot out of Horace's rear and bounced in front of them. Hank swerved just as the little whatever-it-was exploded.

"What the . . . ? Grenades?!"

And another one fired, forcing them to swerve again. *BOOM!* It exploded just past them on the left.

"He's not trying to beat us," Alex said. "He's trying to kill us!"

The third grenade bounced right onto Herbie's hood. Miraculously, it passed all the way over them and rolled off Herbie's back before exploding on the road behind them. There was a collective sigh of relief.

"This isn't just about winning, Hank," Roddy stated, seriously. "It's about good versus evil, love versus hate. Hate can't win, Hank. It just can't."

"Nothing like a little pressure," Hank replied, stepping hard on the gas.

Herbie rocketed ahead, passing Horace and moving directly in front of him.

"They're passing us," Rupert reported.

"I know that, Rupert."

"You're *letting* them pass us."

"I know that as well, Rupert."

The finish line was now in sight, and it actually looked as though Herbie was going to win.

"Is that it? The finish line?" Hank asked, surprised.

Alex smiled. "Are you stunned you might actually win?"

"You're driving like a champ, Hank," Roddy added.

"You really are," Alex agreed. "But hey," she continued, "if you don't want to ruin your record, you could always just pull over here."

Hank glanced in the mirror and saw Horace closing in.

"Not just yet . . ."

Inside the evil car, Simon was preparing for modification number three. There wasn't much time. The finish line was only a short distance away.

"Not modification number three!" Rupert cried, his voice shaking.

"Yes indeed, Rupert. Ready yourself!"

They both put on their protective goggles as Simon prepared to give Rupert the signal.

"What are they doing back there?" Alex asked.

"I don't know," Hank replied. "But I don't think we're going to like it."

"FIRE!" Simon shouted, and Rupert flipped the switch marked "Mod #3."

Horace shook violently as a low rumble came from deep inside him, rising to a high-pitched wail. From a small opening on Horace's hood, a red beam shot across the empty space between the two cars and centered on Herbie just at the base of his rear hatch. It was a laser, and it was burning straight through Herbie and out the other side.

"He really has seen too many James Bond movies," Alex said.

"Just hold together, Herbie. Only a little ways to go."

The laser was slicing Herbie in half. Alex shifted around in the back seat, trying to get out of the beam's way. Seconds later the beam was through the roof, and with that, Herbie split in half, leaving Alex straddled in the center, hanging on for dear life.

"Pick a side, Alex!" Hank shouted as Alex grabbed onto the headrest and pulled herself in with Hank. Roddy, on the other hand, was sprawled against the right side window, terrified.

With several feet of road between them, Hank and Alex looked curiously at Roddy. This wasn't, after all, something that happened every day.

"How American of them," Simon said, grinning. "They've become a drive-thru."

And with that, he stepped on the gas and started to make his way between Herbie's two halves.

Herbie beeped a chorus of *"EEP-EEP-EEP-*

EEP, EEP EEP!" and somehow managed to cause his right side to speed up.

The finish line was very close now, and Simon was surprised to see a group of people, photographers and others, waving and cheering underneath a banner that read CAR AND TRACK SALUTES THE WINNER.

"What the . . . ?"

"You're gonna be on the cover of my magazine," Alex shouted to him. "As the"—she made an L with her thumb and index finger—"LOSER!"

Simon turned his attention back to the road in front of him. Herbie's right half was still ahead. In fact, Herbie's right half, with a terrified Roddy clinging inside, was going to win.

The crowd cheered as the cars shot past the finish line, Herbie's right half first, then Horace, then Herbie's left half.

With flashbulbs popping and pictures snapping, Hank, Alex, and a somewhat dazed Roddy shared a group hug in the winner's circle as Herbie's two halves faced outward next to each other.

"I guess you and I have some more welding to do," Hank laughed at Roddy.

"Hank, you almost won," Alex joked, kissing him.

"Herbie won," Hank said, smiling happily, "and that's all that really matters."

As Horace skidded to a stop, Simon climbed out, fuming.

"I hate that little car," he growled.

But Horace wasn't finished. Watching Herbie's two halves celebrating with the reporters, watching Hank and Alex twirling each other around and kissing, it was all starting to boil his oil. Recklessly, he sped off toward them, as Simon and Rupert watched in amazement.

"Look out!" Hank shouted as he and Roddy grabbed halves of Herbie and moved them out of the way.

It was too late for Horace to stop, and he shot through the scattering crowd, speeding straight for the cliff. Simon and Rupert watched in horror as Horace soared off the embankment, plunging several hundred feet into the gorge below. They ran to the edge just in time to see a fiery explosion, punctuated by flying debris and billowing smoke.

Simon looked away and slowly wiped what he thought was a tear from his eye, but thankfully, it was only a speck of dust.

At the same time, a patrol car pulled to a stop and two officers, directed by the assembled crowd, approached Simon and Rupert.

"That your vehicle?" one of the officer's asked, pointing over the cliff.

"The dead one?" Simon answered. "Yes, what about it?"

The officer removed a pad from his shirt pocket and began writing. "Felony detonation of explosives, illegal possession of an unregistered wild vehicle, misdemeanor dumping of said vehicle . . ."

"So what are you saying?" Simon asked stupidly.

"You're going to jail," he said, spinning Simon around and slapping on the cuffs. "But consider yourself lucky. You already have a cellmate."

The other officer grabbed Rupert, and the four of them started off toward the idling patrol car. They stopped briefly in front of Hank and Alex.

"I'll get you for this, Cooper," Simon said angrily, "and your stupid Bug!" Then he turned his attention to Alex. "Hey Alex," he said, trying to look irresistible. "I'll give you call."

"You're only allowed one," Alex fired back. Everyone laughed as the officers dragged Rupert and Simon away.

Just then, Chuck's El Camino coasted to a

stop alongside them and died. Chuck hurried out of the car, knowing full well that whatever had happened was over.

"What'd I miss?"

Hank, Alex, and Roddy looked at each other, then at Chuck, and when they couldn't hold it in any longer, they burst out laughing.

CHAPTER EIGHT

"Say 'Herbie'!"

"HERBIE!" the group said together as the photographer snapped the picture. It was several weeks later, Herbie was all fixed up, and Alex was putting the finishing touches on her article.

"The men in Herbie's life," she said to herself as she looked at Hank, Roddy, Jim Douglas, and Dr. Stumpfel standing together.

"Okay," Alex said, professionally, "it's a wrap."

They had been shooting all day, including the magazine-cover shot of a newly wed couple in full wedding attire standing in Herbie's sunroof. Hank had commented how good Alex would look in a wedding gown, a suggestion that hadn't gone unnoticed.

"So where are we going tonight?" Alex asked as she took Hank's hand and walked with him toward Herbie.

"Dunno," he said. "Herbie hasn't told me yet."

They were about to get into the car when they heard Jim Douglas's voice.

"Before you go," Jim said, walking toward them. "I just wanted to know. What are you going to call this article?"

Hank and Alex shared a knowing glance.

"Well," Alex summarized, "I was thinking of calling it 'The Love Bug.' "

" 'The Love Bug.' *Hmm.*" Jim considered it thoughtfully. "I like it!"

"Eeeerrreeep!" Herbie agreed.

Then, with a bleating chorus of "Here Comes the Bride," Herbie opened his door and let the couple get into the backseat. Without hesitation, they began to kiss. Herbie would be their chauffeur for the night, and it was a good thing, too. They were still kissing when he made the turn toward Seabreeze Point.

"REER EREEEP!" Herbie beeped happily as he raced up the narrow road.

Mission accomplished.

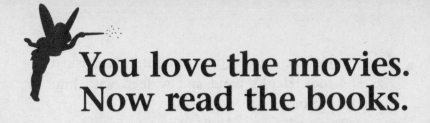

You love the movies. Now read the books.

Toy Story

The hilarious tale of toys that come to life, and a special friendship.

starring
Tom Hanks
Tim Allen

Tower of Terror

In 1939, five partygoers disappeared from a hotel elevator on their way up to the penthouse for a Halloween party. Can this chilling mystery be solved today by reenacting the fateful ride?

starring
Steve Guttenberg
Kirsten Dunst

Cinderella

The classic tale of romance and sibling rivalry retold with an all-star cast.

starring
Whitney Houston
Whoopi Goldberg
Brandy
Jason Alexander

The Santa Clause

When Scott Calvin puts on Santa's red suit, his life is changed . . . forever.

starring
Tim Allen

The Love Bug

Herbie's back in an all-new adventure that includes his evil twin, "Horace, the Hate Bug"!

Ruby Bridges

The true story of six-year-old Ruby Bridges, one of the first African-American students to integrate public schools in New Orleans.

**At Bookstores
Everywhere**

The Wonderful World of Disney

Recapture the magic!

© Disn

Make Sunday nights special with **The Wonderful World of Disney**

Your Favorite Films . . . Your Favorite Stars

Aladdin and the King of Thieves
Angels in the End Zone
Babe
Billy Madison
Casper
Cinderella
Empty Tigers
Flash
The Garbage-Picking,
   Field Goal-Kicking
   Philadelphia Phenomenon
Gold Rush
House Guest
Jungle Book
The Lion King
A Little Princess
The Little Rascals
Look Who's Talking Now
The Love Bug
Miracle at Midnight
My Date with the President's
   Daughter
Oliver Twist
Pocahontas
The Principal Takes a Holiday
Ruby Bridges
Sabrina the Teen Witch
Safety Patrol
The Santa Clause
Swapping Sam
Toothless
Tourist Trap
Tower of Terror
Toy Story

Whitney Houston
Whoopi Goldberg
Brandy
Richard Dreyfuss
Alyssa Milano
Christopher Lloyd
Kirstie Alley
Leslie Nielsen
Kirsten Dunst
Tony Danza
Tim Allen
Tom Hanks
Steve Guttenberg
Jason Alexander
Elijah Wood
and many more!

Watch every Sunday night on abc

© Disney